T0353803

Lovey Dove Flies to Europe

Carlene Brod & Morris Chalick

To order additional copies of this book, contact:
Xlibris
844-714-8691
www.Xlibris.com
Orders@Xlibris.com

ISBN:	Softcover	979-8-3694-2809-2
	Hardcover	979-8-3694-2810-8
	EBook	979-8-3694-2808-5

Library of Congress Control Number: 2024917309

Print information available on the last page

Rev. date: 08/19/2024

Lovey Dove Flies to Europe

HELLO LOVEY DOVE

LOVEY DOVE FLIES OVER THE ATLANTIC OCEAN

FIRST STOP; ICELAND, A NORTHERN ISLAND
COUNTRY WITH BEAUTIFUL LANDSCAPES

FROM THE COLD COUNTRY, LOVEY DOVE
FLIES TO A BEAUTIFUL GARDEN IN LONDON

LOVEY DOVE WANTS TO SEE BUCKINGHAM PALACE WHERE THE KING AND QUEEN LIVE

THIS IS A CROWN FOR THE KING AND QUEEN

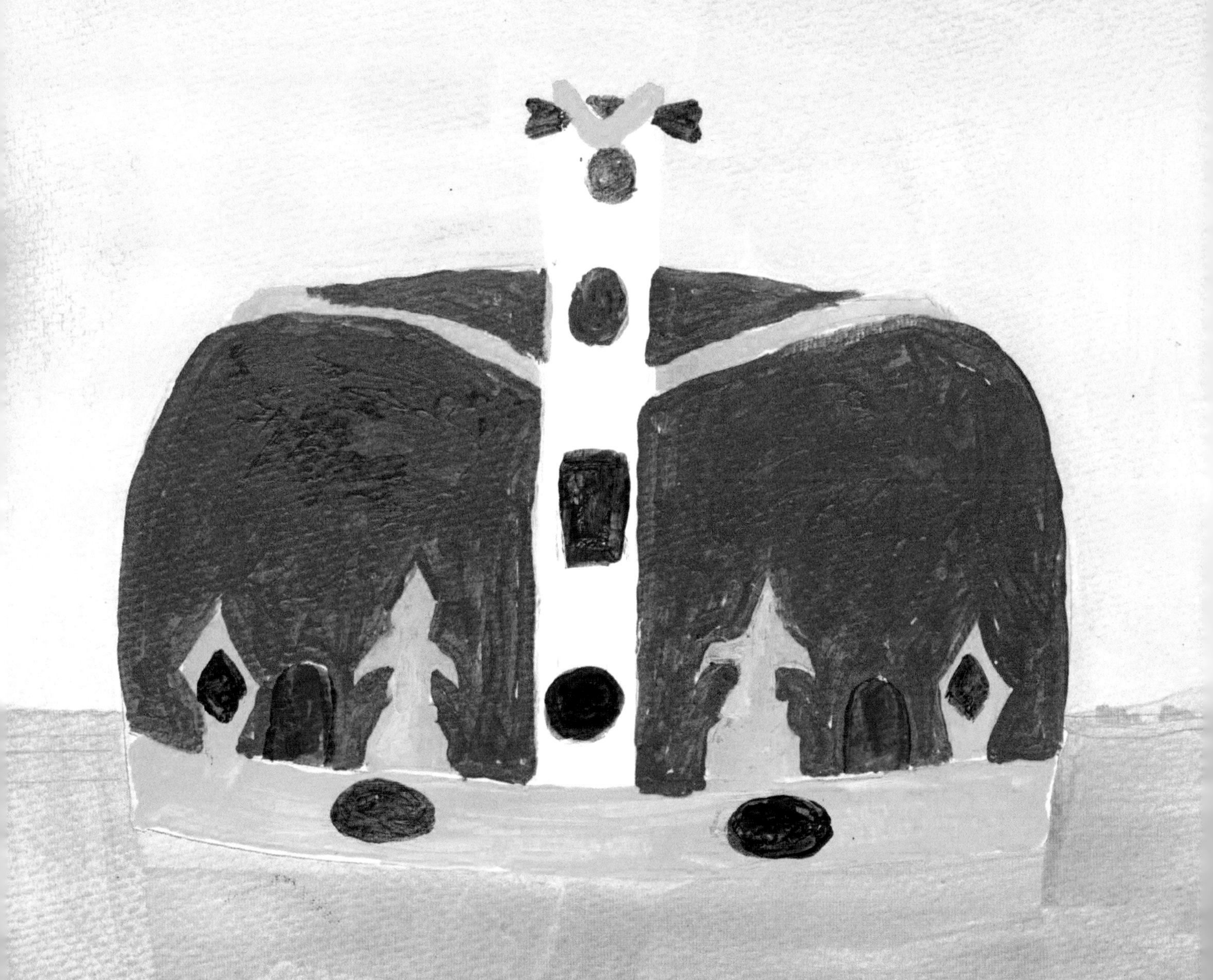

THE NEXT STOP
IS THE FAMOUS
EIFFEL TOWER IN
PARIS, FRANCE

BEAUTIFUL PAINTINGS WERE MADE IN MONET'S GARDEN IN FRANCE

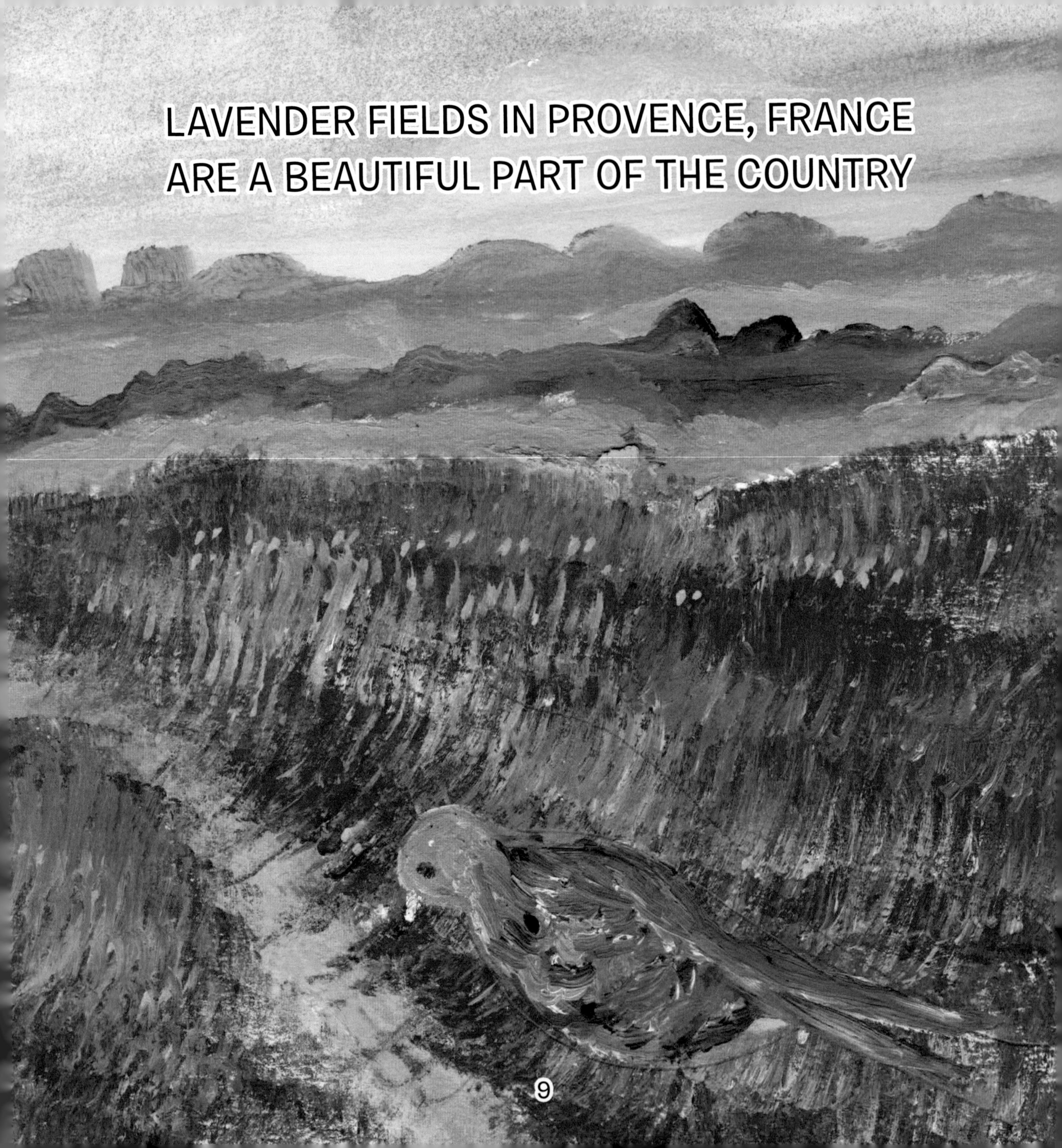

LAVENDER FIELDS IN PROVENCE, FRANCE ARE A BEAUTIFUL PART OF THE COUNTRY

IN BELGIUM, DELICIOUS CHOCOLATES ARE MADE

NEXT STOP FOR LOVEY IS ITALY. LOVEY WANTS TO RIDE A GONDOLA IN VENICE

IN ITALY, THE LEANING TOWER OF PISA STANDS ON UNEVEN GROUND

LOVEY STOPS IN GERMANY WHERE MANY CARS ARE MADE

IN THE NETHERLANDS, THERE ARE MORE THAN 1000 WINDMILLS. THE BLADES HELP MAKE ENERGY FROM THE WIND

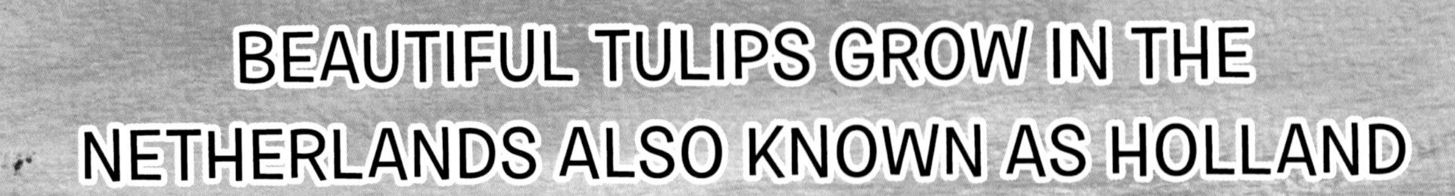

BEAUTIFUL TULIPS GROW IN THE NETHERLANDS ALSO KNOWN AS HOLLAND

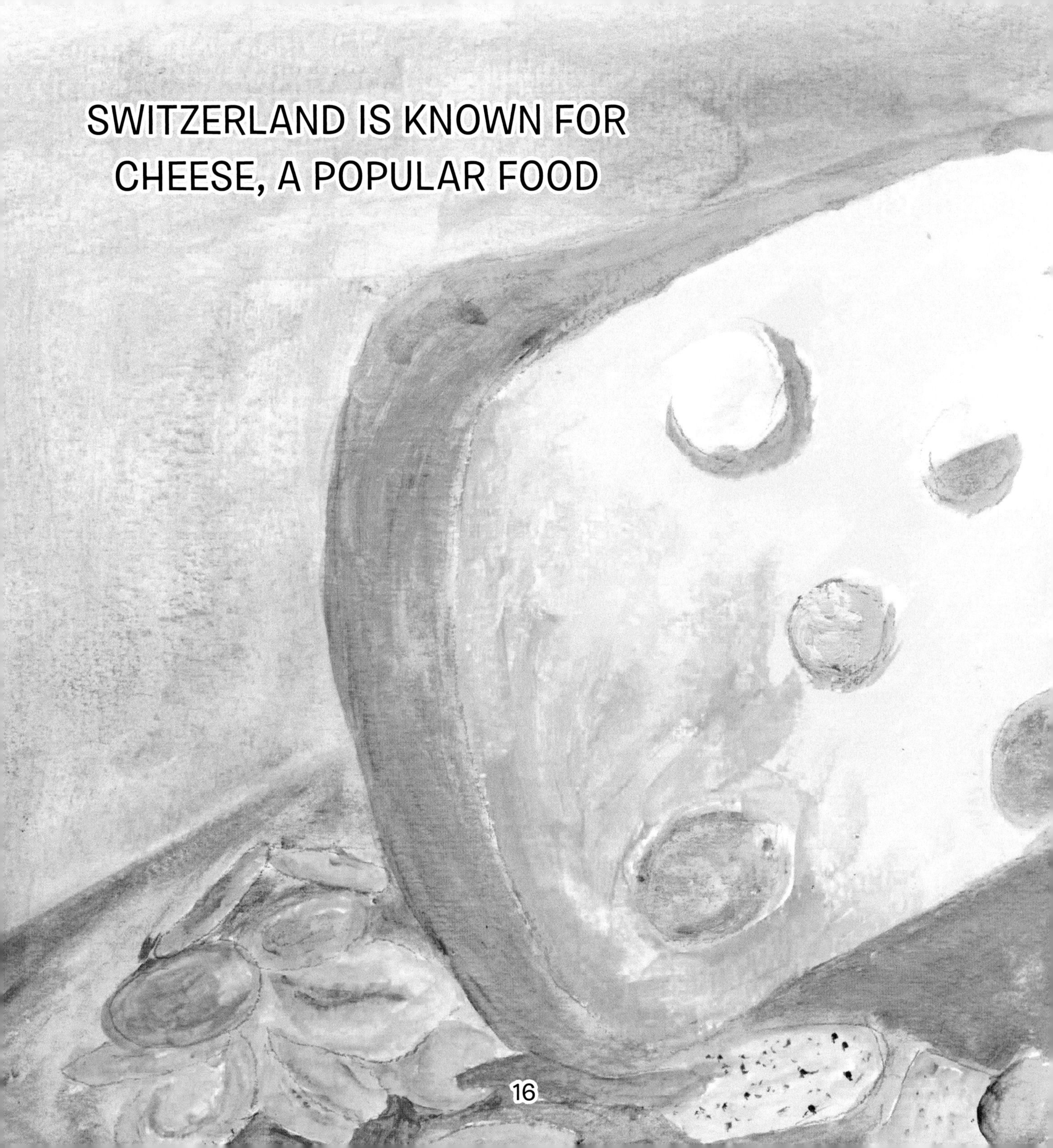

SWITZERLAND IS KNOWN FOR CHEESE, A POPULAR FOOD

SWISS MOUNTAINS ARE BEAUTIFUL AND FAMOUS FOR SKIING

MANY FAMOUS
MUSICIANS WROTE
MUSIC IN AUSTRIA

SPAIN IS KNOWN FOR FAMOUS DANCING

Printed in the United States
by Baker & Taylor Publisher Services

GREECE IS WHERE THE OLYMPIC GAMES BEGAN

LOVEY DOVE WILL RETURN TO THE UNITED STATES OF AMERICA AFTER THE TRIP

EUROPE
Iceland
Norwegian Sea
Faroe Islands
Shetland Islands
Orkney Islands
Hebrides
North Sea
Norway
Sweden
Finland
Gulf of Bothnia
Baltic Sea
Gotland
Öland
Estonia
Latvia
Lithuania
Russia
Belarus
Denmark
Ireland
Isle of Man
United Kingdom
Netherlands
Belgium
Germany
Poland
Ukraine
Czech Republic
Slovakia
Austria
Hungary
Moldova
Romania
Switzerland
Slovenia
Croatia
France
Bay of Biscay
Monaco
Andorra
Spain
Portugal
Corsica
Sardinia
Italy
Bosnia and Herzegovina
Serbia
Kosovo
Montenegro
Albania
Macedonia
Bulgaria
Black Sea
Greece
Aegean Sea
Turkey
Ionian Sea
Corfu
Lefkada
Kefalonia
Zakynthos
Crete
Tyrrhenian Sea
Majorca
Menorca
Ibiza
Balearic Islands
Formentera
Mediterranean Sea
Sicily
Malta
Gibraltar
North Atlantic Ocean
Morocco
Algeria
Tunisia
Lovingly made by Bigjigs Toys

CONTRIBUTORS TO LOVEY DOVE BOOK

BROD, BRUCE
BROD, GARY
BROD, ROY
DUBE, TAMMY
GROB, LIAM
PAPSUN, DONNA
SCARGILL, NETTA